Down in a submarine we'll go—
under the sea, way down below,
where fishes swim and
porpoises play.
Now off we go—we're underway!

Mike Berenstain

Based on the characters created by
Stan and Jan Berenstain

An Imprint of HarperCollins*Publishers*

 For information address HarperCollins Children's Books, a division of HarperCollins Publishers, 195 Broadway, New York, NY 10007. www.harpercollinschildrens.com
Library of Congress Control Number: 2015935863 ISBN 978-0-06-235011-4
20 21 CWM 10 9 ❖ First Edition

The Bear family was visiting one of their favorite places—the Bear Country Aquarium. They were having a fine time watching the dolphins leap and the seals catch fish.

They saw otters and penguins dive and play. They saw different kinds of colorful fish and other interesting sea creatures like octopuses and jellyfish.

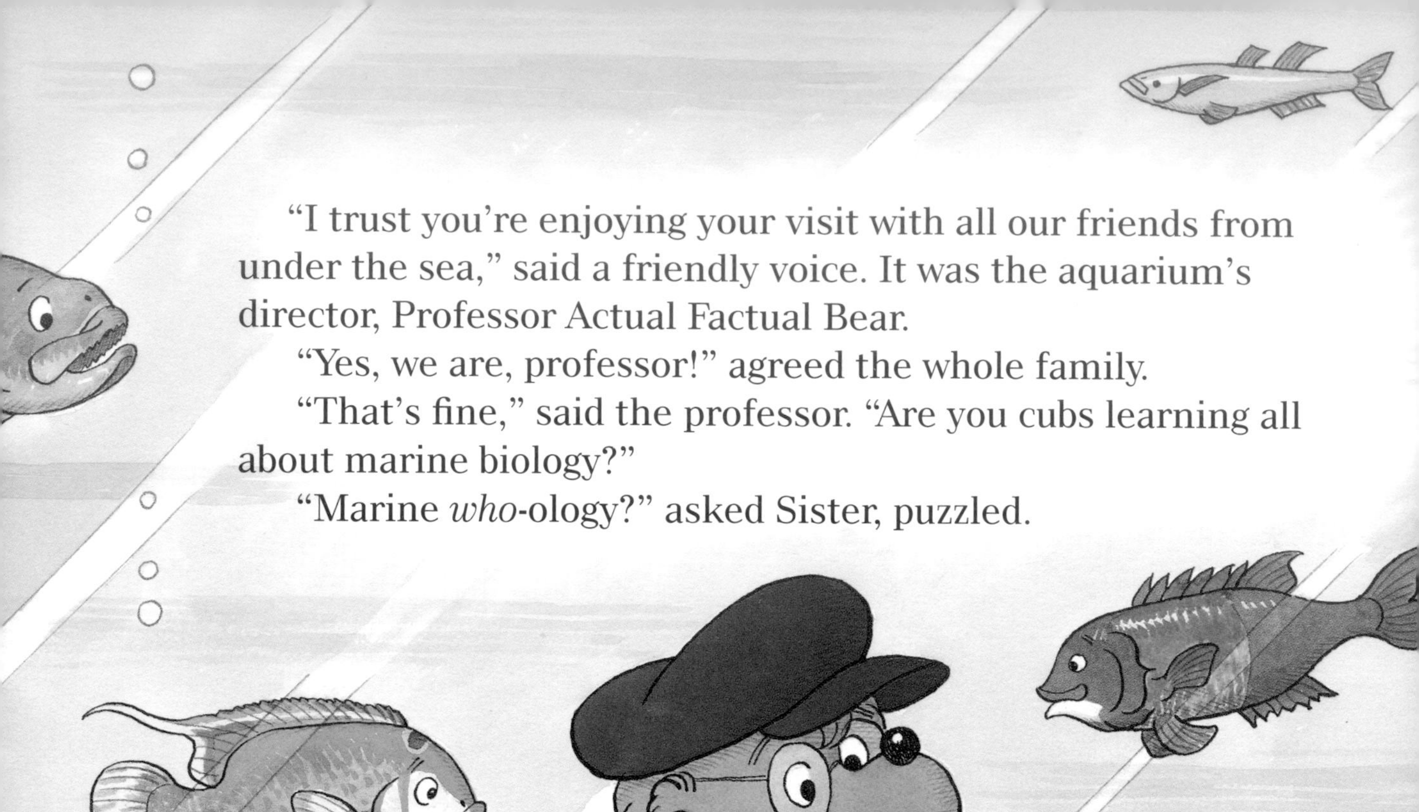

"I trust you're enjoying your visit with all our friends from under the sea," said a friendly voice. It was the aquarium's director, Professor Actual Factual Bear.

"Yes, we are, professor!" agreed the whole family.

"That's fine," said the professor. "Are you cubs learning all about marine biology?"

"Marine *who*-ology?" asked Sister, puzzled.

“Marine *bi*-ology!” The professor laughed. “That just means the study of things that live in the sea.”

“Yes,” said Sister, “but it seems a shame we can only see these creatures in tanks and pools. It would be wonderful to see them where they really live—under the sea!”

“As a matter of fact,” the professor said, “we *can* go see them in their natural habitat.”

“Their natural habi-*what*?” asked Brother.

“Where they really live—under the sea,” said the professor. “Just come with me.”

“This is my Deep-Diver Submarine,” said the professor.

“Wow!” said Brother.

“Terrific!” said Sister.

“Would you like to come aboard for a little trip—down under the sea?”

“Yes!” they all said. “We would!”

“Then climb aboard,” said the professor.

The submarine was soon underway, sailing on the surface of the Great Bear Country Ocean.

"The ocean surface is the feeding ground for many seabirds," explained the professor. "Seagulls, terns, pelicans, cormorants, and ospreys swoop and dive to catch the fish they eat."

"Look!" said Sister. "There's something jumping."

"Those are flying fish," said the professor. "They leap out of the water and spread their fins to glide away from danger."

"And there's the danger!" said Papa.

"Yes," said the professor, "a pod of dolphins."

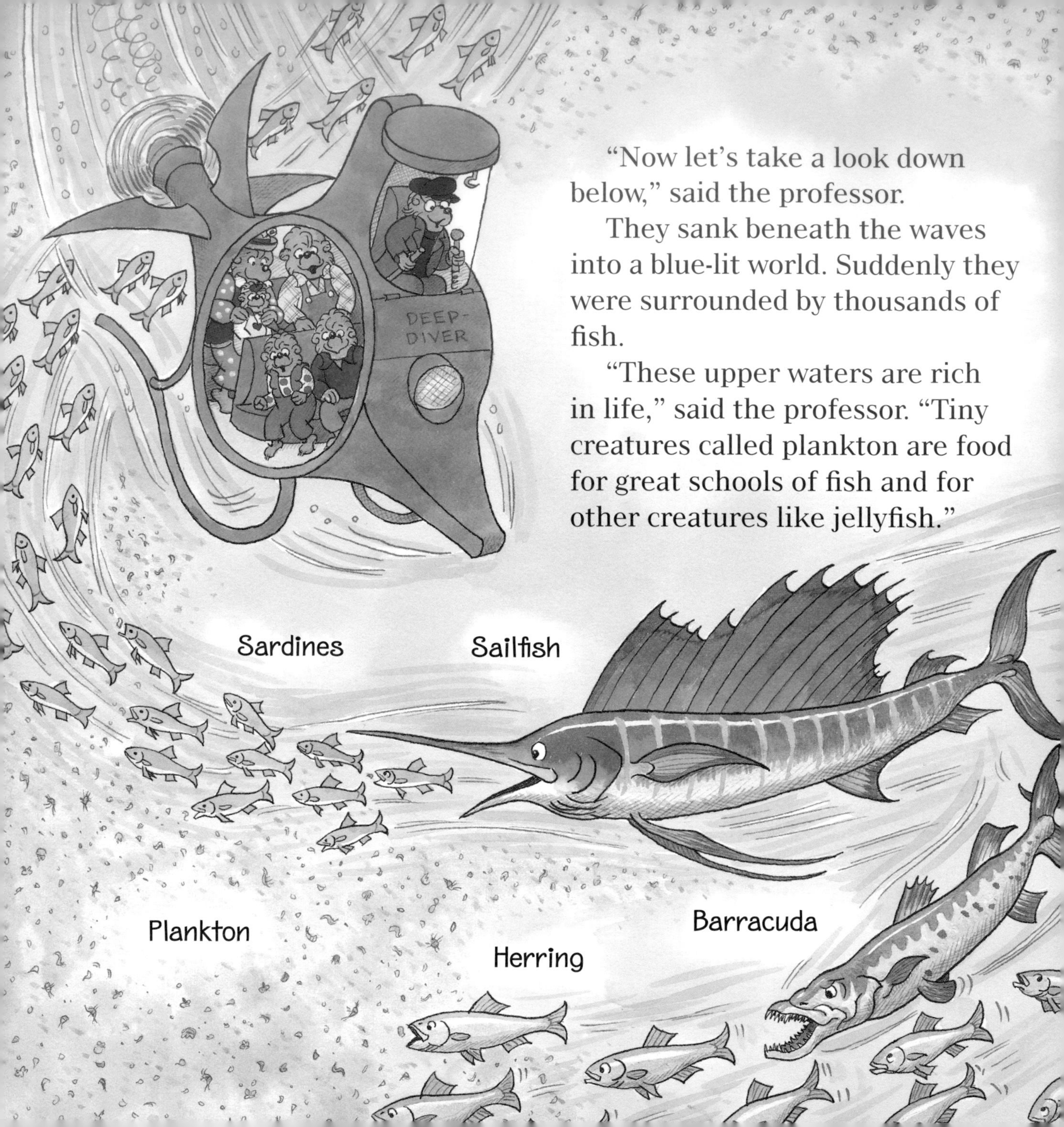

"Now let's take a look down below," said the professor.

They sank beneath the waves into a blue-lit world. Suddenly they were surrounded by thousands of fish.

"These upper waters are rich in life," said the professor. "Tiny creatures called plankton are food for great schools of fish and for other creatures like jellyfish."

"Look!" said Brother. "Sharks!"

"Yes," said the professor. "Big fish like sharks feed on little fish that feed on plankton."

“Some of the largest sea creatures feed on tiny plankton, too,” said the professor. “Manta rays, whale sharks, and even the largest creature of them all—the great blue whale.”

“Look!” said Sister. “That whale has a baby.”

“Oh my!” said Mama. “What a big baby!”

“Cute, though!” said Papa.

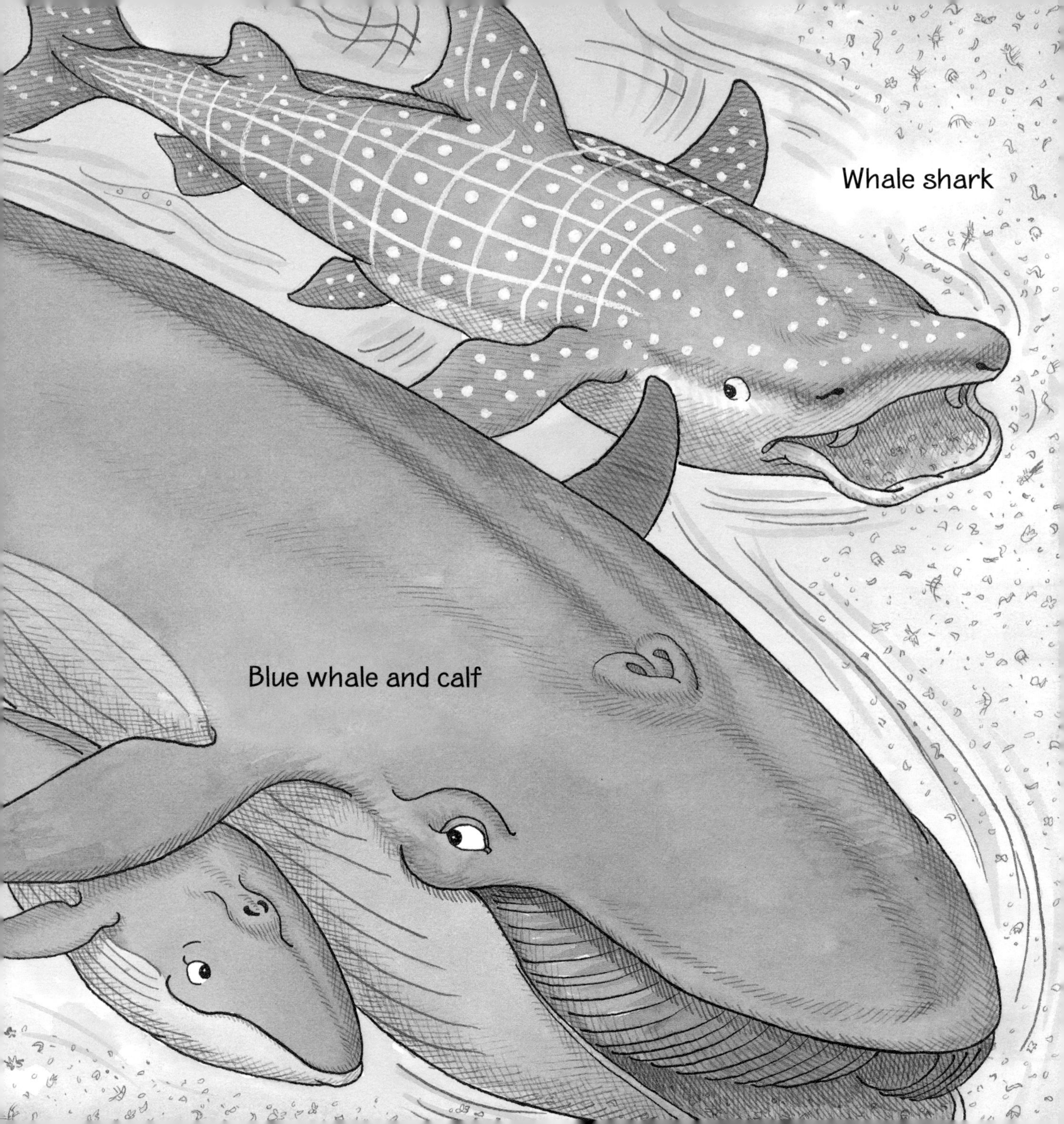
Whale shark
Blue whale and calf

"Along the coast we come to a coral reef," said the professor. "It is built by tiny creatures and is rich in life. All who live here have ways to protect themselves. The anemone looks like a flower but is really an animal with stingers in its arms. The stingers don't hurt the clown fish, which hides in the anemone for safety. A puffer fish blows itself up like a balloon to keep from being eaten.

“Stingrays have poisonous stingers in their tails. The octopus squirts a cloud of ink and changes color to confuse its enemies.”

“What a clever critter!” said Brother.

"Now it's time to explore the deeper waters," said the professor. "It gets dark down here, so we'll switch on our lights. Not too many creatures live at this depth. But those that do can be very big, such as the giant squid—the favorite food of another giant: the sperm whale, which dives down to battle its prey!"

"Wow!" said Sister. "They're humongous!"

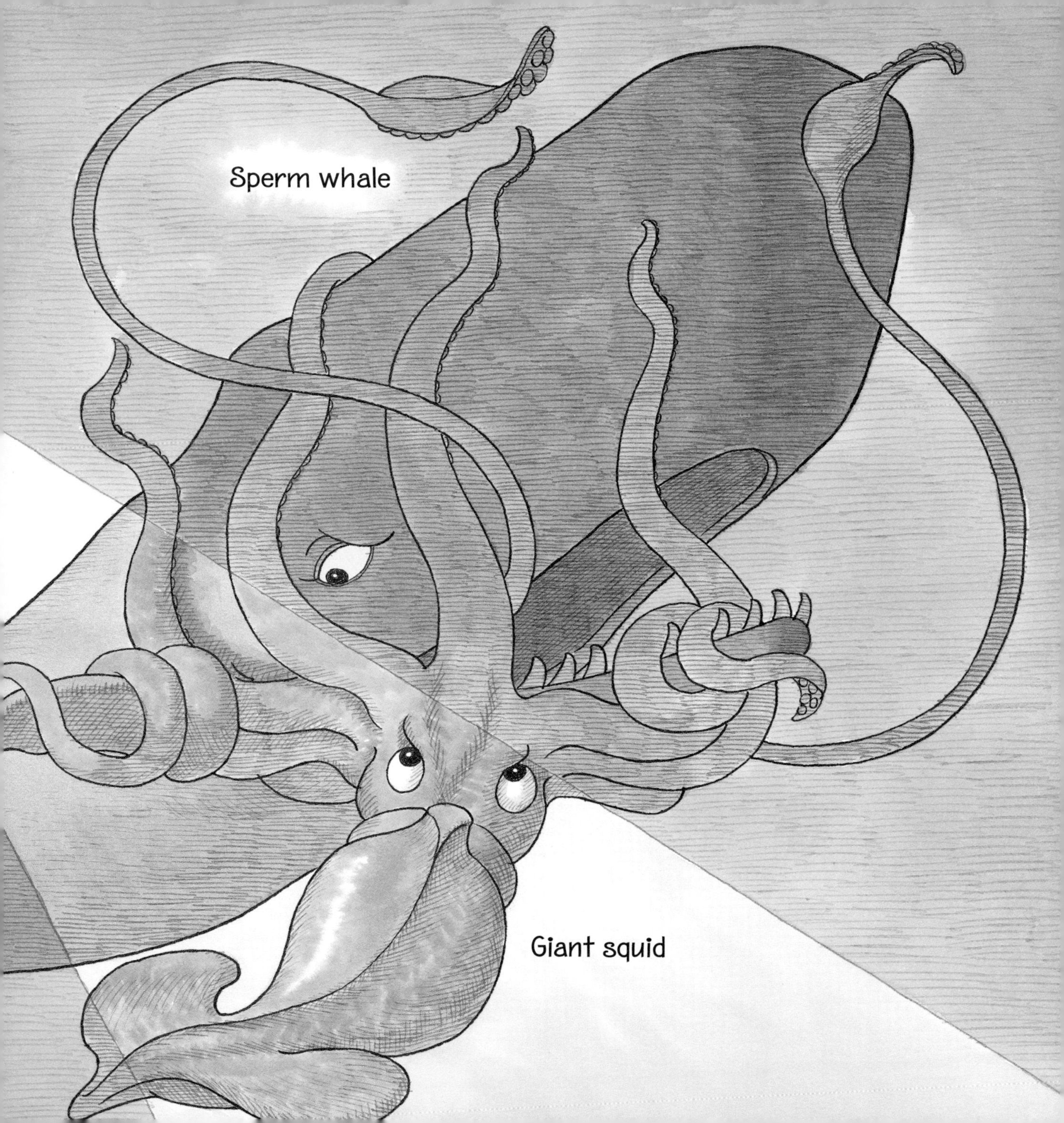
Sperm whale
Giant squid

"As we go even deeper, the sea creatures get stranger and stranger. It's so dark they have to make their own light—like the anglerfish, which waves a light to lure fish into its jaws. Some of the fish here have enormous teeth and can swallow their prey whole. Some just look really weird!"
"I'll say!" said Brother. "Ugh!"
Hatchetfish
Anglerfish
Lantern fish
DEEP-DIVER

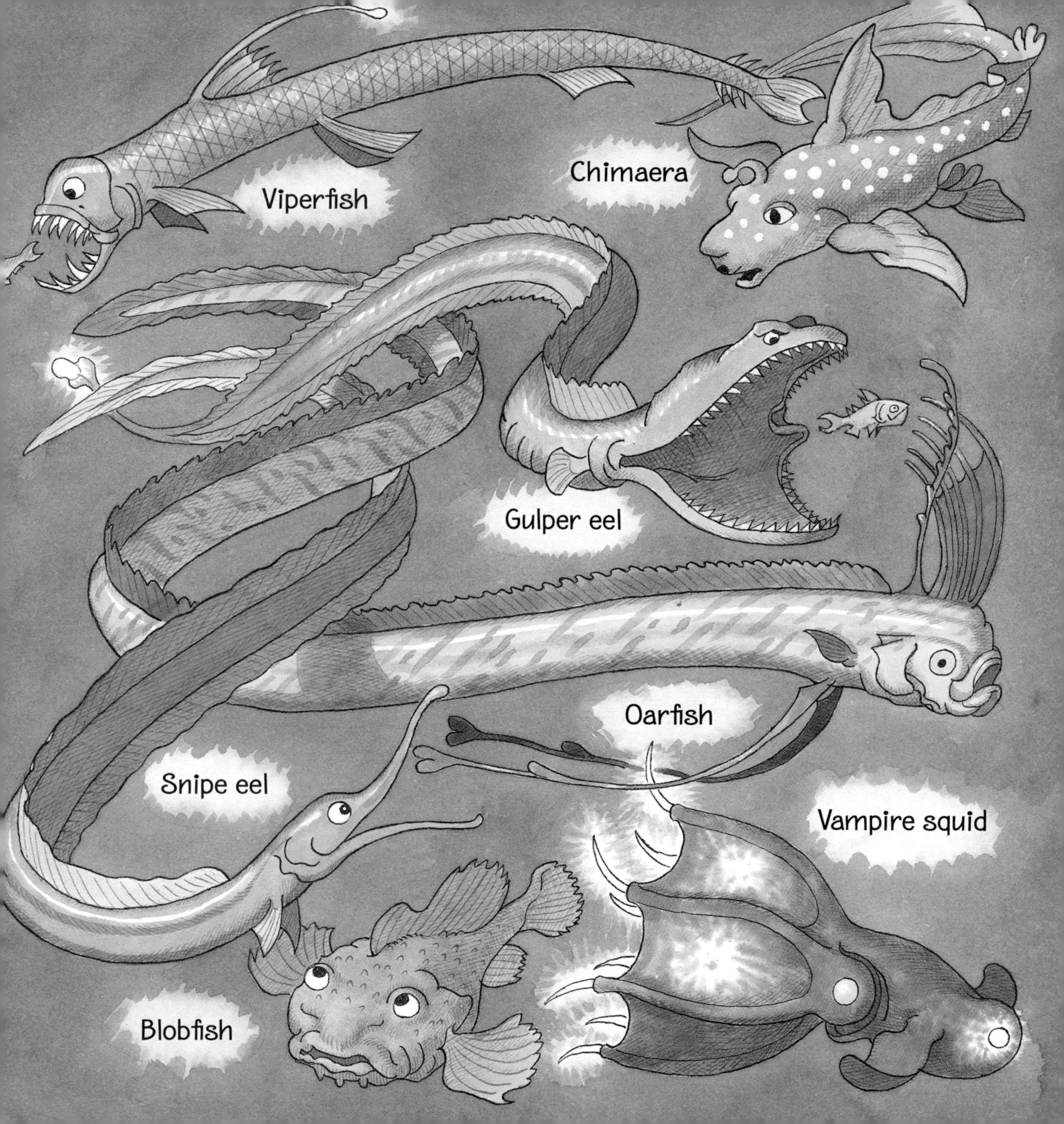
Viperfish
Chimaera
Gulper eel
Oarfish
Snipe eel
Vampire squid
Blobfish

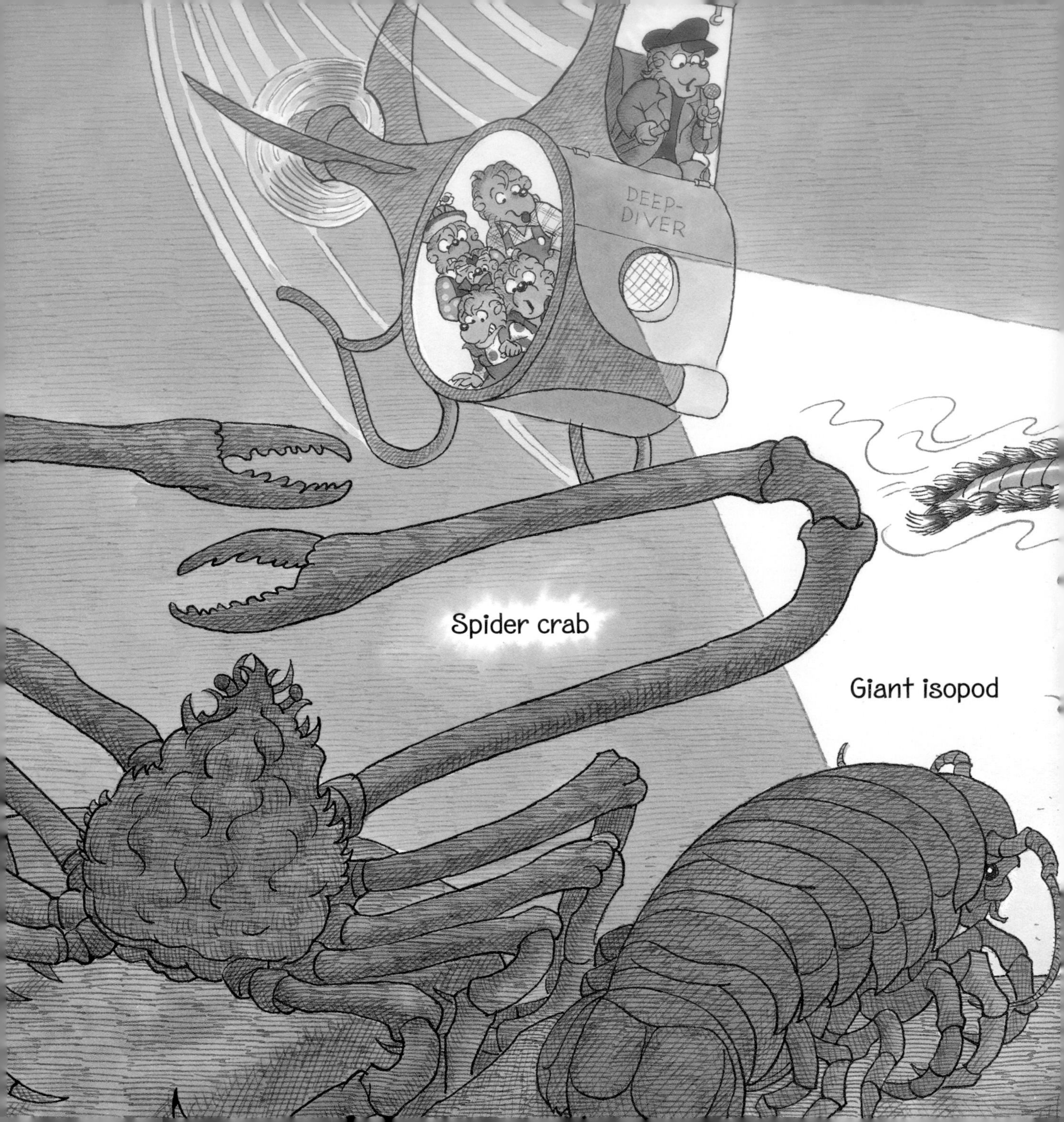
DEEP-
DIVER
Spider crab
Giant isopod

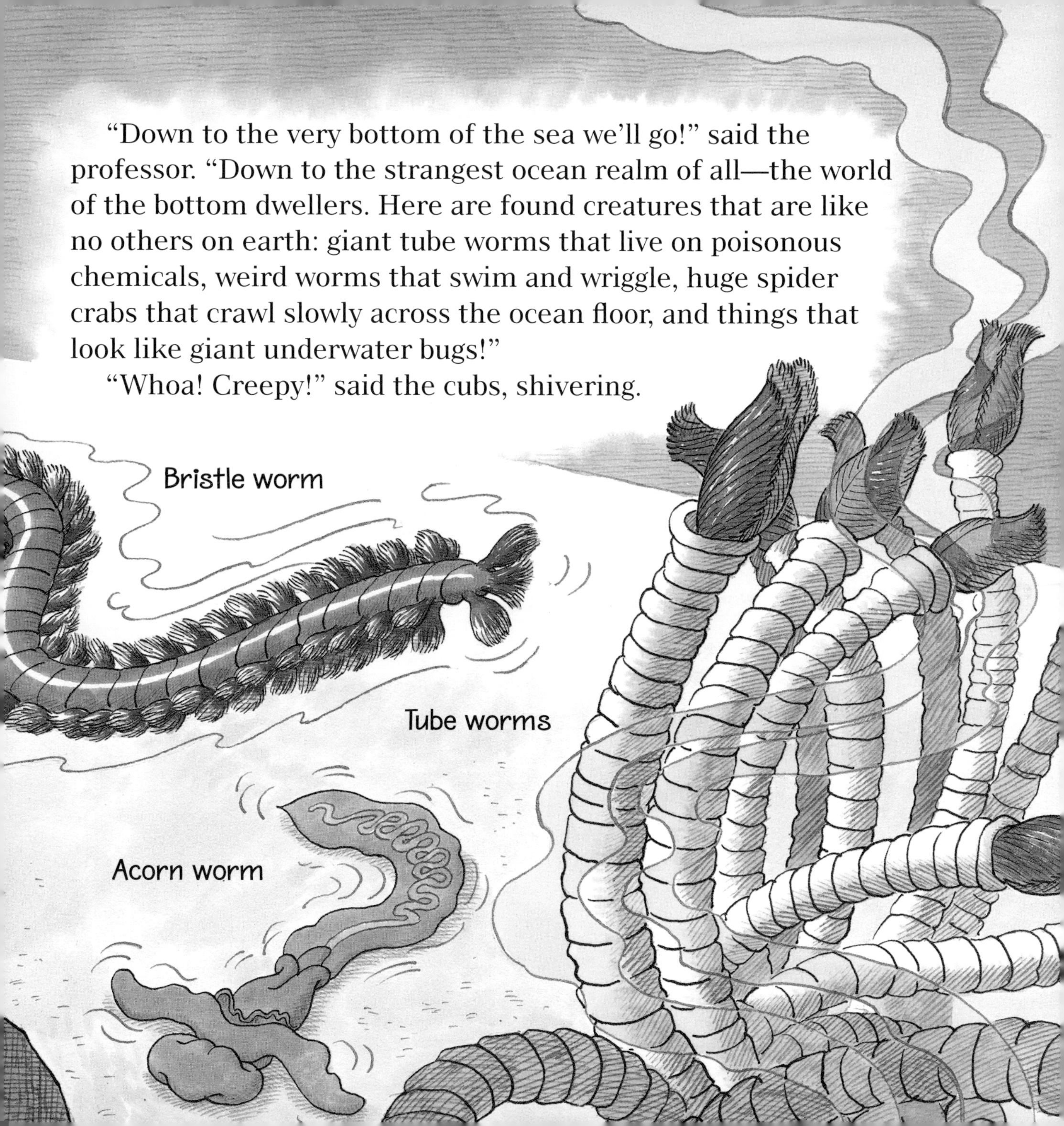

"Down to the very bottom of the sea we'll go!" said the professor. "Down to the strangest ocean realm of all—the world of the bottom dwellers. Here are found creatures that are like no others on earth: giant tube worms that live on poisonous chemicals, weird worms that swim and wriggle, huge spider crabs that crawl slowly across the ocean floor, and things that look like giant underwater bugs!"

"Whoa! Creepy!" said the cubs, shivering.

"But now," said the professor, "it's time to return to the surface and say good-bye to all our undersea friends."

As he steered the submarine upward, the Bear family peered out the submarine's ports and waved good-bye to all the strange, interesting, and beautiful creatures of the deep they had seen.

“Thank you, professor!” said Papa as they went ashore. “That was a wonderful trip.”

“Yes!” agreed Mama. “We all learned so much.”

“I’ll say!” said Sister. “I think I really *do* want to be a marine bio . . . uh . . . marine bio-thingy . . . um . . .” She scratched her head. “Well, I want to be just like you, professor!”

“Thank you, Sister,” said the professor, shaking her hand. “That’s the best compliment I’ve ever had.”

“You’re welcome,” said Sister. “And I just can’t wait to go back down under the sea!”